The Boxcar Children Mysteries

THE MIDNIGHT MYSTERY

created by
GERTRUDE CHANDLER WARNER

Illustrated by Hodges Soileau

SCHOLASTIC INC.
New York Toronto London Auckland Sydney
New Delhi Mexico City Hong Kong Buenos Aires

ISBN 0-439-51748-6

12 11 10 9 8 7 6 5 4 3 2   3 4 5 6 7 8/0

Printed in the U.S.A.   40
First Scholastic printing, July 2003

Contents

Contents

CHAPTER 1

Benny's Flashlight Hat

"It's too dark in the backseat to play magnetic checkers," Henry Alden grumbled. "I can hardly see any of my black pieces."

"That's because I jumped most of them," his brother, Benny, answered.

Henry frowned. Like the other Aldens, Henry was usually cheerful on family car trips. But here he was, fourteen years old and losing at checkers to his six-year-old brother. "I'm no match for Benny and his flashlight hat," he admitted.

The two brothers, along with their two sisters, Jessie and Violet, had been riding in Grandfather Alden's car for hours. Now it was dark and not a good time to play car games. But Benny could see fine, thanks to the new invention he wore on his head. On other nighttime car trips, Benny had wished for a hat with a built-in flashlight so he could see and have both hands free to play car games. When Grandfather's friend Isabel Putter invited the whole family to take part in the invention convention she organized every year, Benny knew just what to invent.

"Maybe I could invent a flashlight hat for you, too," Benny offered. He sat back, waiting for Henry to make a tricky move in the dim light of the car.

Henry groaned. "You rascal! You're probably going to beat me at checkers *and* win first prize at the invention convention with your hat."

"Hope so." Benny smiled confidently.

To make the hat even more useful, Benny had attached a mirror to it. Violet, who was ten, had found an old dental mirror in her crafts bag, which was full of odds and ends. She and Benny had attached the small mirror-on-a-stick to the flashlight hat. Not only could Benny see in the dark, he could see what was behind him, too!

Twelve-year-old Jessie didn't need a flashlight hat. She always remembered to bring along a plain old flashlight to read maps in the car at night. "Good thing there's a full moon tonight," Jessie said as they drove past the building she'd been looking for. "I think that was the Red Rooster Diner, Grandfather. Ms. Putter said to look for the big wooden rooster on the roof and take the next right."

"You're an excellent navigator, Jessie," Mr. Alden said as he made the right turn. "Sorry we left Greenfield so late. I'm afraid we won't arrive much before midnight. Not to worry, though. Isabel said she would wait up for us."

Mr. Alden looked thoughtful. "It's a shame Isabel's grandmother, Alice Putter, didn't live long enough to see how Isabel has turned the invention convention into such a big event. Inventors come from all over."

"Even Greenfield," Benny said, as if they had driven across the world.

A few minutes later, Mr. Alden parked the car at the end of a long driveway. Several bright porch lights came on. The Aldens found themselves facing one of the most curious houses they had ever seen.

"All the windows have different shapes," Violet said. "And the chimneys, too. It looks like a cartoon house."

"I think it looks like a gingerbread house that's melting," Benny said.

Mr. Alden laughed. "Even houses remind you of food, Benny!"

The children could hardly wait to go inside. The house had many doors, each one a different size. The porch wasn't like the one at Grandfather's house, with its straight railings and steps. No, this porch went up, down, and all around the house on different levels.

A concert of barking dogs greeted the Aldens as they opened the car doors.

"Those two dogs look like sausages with legs," Benny said. "Their bellies practically touch the ground."

Jessie giggled as the dogs waddled toward the car. A tall, graceful woman about Grandfather's age walked behind the two basset hounds. "I'm so glad Ms. Putter has dogs, since we had to leave poor Watch at home."

Grandfather smiled. "Poor Watch? Oh, I wouldn't worry about him. You know how Mrs. McGregor spoils him when we're away. She's not only the best housekeeper, but the best dog keeper, too. Watch probably had steak for dinner."

The children hopped out of the car. They were eager to meet Isabel Putter and her dogs.

"Meet Ruff and Tumble," Isabel said. "Ruff is the noisy one. Tumble got his name because he often tumbled off his dog bed when he was a puppy."

Violet giggled as one of the hounds

sniffed at her feet. "They must smell our dog, Watch, on me, Ms. Putter. He slept on my sneakers last night."

"Careful," Isabel warned. "Their favorite treats are shoelaces. Be sure to put your sneakers in the closet at night." Isabel smoothed her white hair, then buttoned her woolly sweater over her bathrobe. "Please excuse my nightclothes. I wasn't sure when you'd be arriving. I'm certainly glad to meet you children. You weren't even born yet when your parents visited a long time ago."

The children were quiet for a few seconds. They would always miss their parents. Thank goodness for Grandfather. After their parents had died, Henry, Jessie, Violet, and Benny, plus Watch, had lived by themselves in a boxcar in the woods. Grandfather had searched all over until he'd found them. Now they lived in Grandfather's big comfy house in Greenfield. And they still had their boxcar, which Grandfather had placed in his backyard for the children to use as a playhouse.

"Whoa!" Benny cried as Ruff and Tumble ran after a raccoon in the nearby garden. "Who's that standing in your garden? I mean, *what's* that?"

Everyone turned to look. Smack in the middle of the garden, next to several tomato plants, stood the tall, wiry shape of a man.

Isabel Putter laughed. "That, Benny, was Grandma Alice's idea of a scarecrow! I'm sure your grandfather told you that my grandmother was a sculptor and an inventor. Many of her sculptures are beautiful *and* useful. When there's a breeze, that big metal scarecrow spins around and scares the birds and animals from the garden."

"Good thing Ruff and Tumble can't run very fast on their stubby legs," Jessie said as she watched the two dogs trying to catch up to the raccoon. "The Greenfield raccoons know better than to visit Grandfather's house if Watch is around."

Isabel led the Aldens up the steps of the house. She pushed open one of the low doors. "You can go in this one, Benny. Grandma Alice designed doors for grown-ups and doors for children."

"And doors for dogs." Benny lowered his head and entered through the Benny-sized doorway behind Ruff and Tumble, who had given up chasing the raccoon.

When the children stepped into the large entryway, they were startled to see a huge round face staring back at them.

"Whoa!" Henry said. "That's the biggest grandfather clock I've ever seen. Does it work?"

Isabel smiled at the children. "You'll hear it strike midnight soon. Grandma Alice became famous for the clocks she designed and built. Each one is different. Grandma Alice loved anything mechanical — music boxes, jewelry boxes, but especially clocks."

Violet stepped in front of the clock and stared up. "The face is the man in the moon. It's hand-painted with stars and blue sky. I've never seen such a beautiful clock."

Isabel came over and stood next to Violet. "I'm glad you like it. Your grandfather told me you're an artist, too. I have to warn you that Grandma Alice had quite a sense of humor. This clock and all the others in the house make a terrible racket at midnight and at noon. I promise you won't sleep through it."

"Who would want to?" Jessie asked as she admired the unusual clock.

"Most people who stay here more than one night!" Isabel answered. "Now, we'd better get you upstairs where you'll be staying."

"*Yeow.*"

Everyone looked up. Two green eyes shone from between the stair railings.

"*Yeow,*" the green-eyed creature cried again.

Isabel laughed. "Oh, Midnight, there you are. Well, you'd better go hide under one of the beds. Ruff and Tumble are here."

As the children drew closer, they saw that the green eyes belonged to a pitch-black cat. A second later it vanished into one of the upstairs rooms.

"Midnight usually has the run of this house, since Ruff and Tumble live in my cottage," Isabel said. "But she's not likely to stick around here if the dogs are nearby."

Isabel shooed the dogs away from the bedroom where Midnight had gone to hide.

As the children climbed to the next floor, they found surprises wherever they turned. Grandma Alice had designed her home like a fun house with crooked chairs, curved mirrors, and tipsy steps.

"Here you are," Isabel said when everyone reached the top floor. "Grandma Alice turned the attic into a special room for all of us grandchildren when we visited. You can see from the size of the doors and windows, it's designed for children, especially the youngest ones." She motioned toward a low purple door.

Benny smiled happily. "For once I'm glad to be the smallest."

Isabel nodded at Henry and Jessie, who were taller than the door. "Sorry, you two. The rest of us will have to scrunch down to get in and out. Violet, I think you can scoot under."

As soon as Violet stepped through the door, she felt right at home. Every wall was a different color, as was each piece of furniture. The space was decorated with one-of-a-kind clocks and lamps that clearly had been designed by Alice Putter. The chairs, dressers, tables, and beds were all the same style, but they were each different heights.

Jessie examined one of the beds. "I get it," she said. "The legs on the furniture are like telescopes. You can expand them to make them higher or lower."

Isabel showed the children how to adjust the furniture. "Grandma Alice wanted furniture all grandchildren could use no matter what size they were. She designed everything in here to grow or shrink. Everyone always said she could make a lot of money selling the furniture. But Grandma Alice didn't care a fig about having plenty of money, just plenty of work and plenty of fun."

"Same with us," Henry said. He turned the legs on one of the beds to raise it up. He needed a tall bed because he was nice and tall. After unrolling his sleeping bag, he flopped back on the bed. "Now it's perfect."

Violet adjusted the chest of drawers next

to the bed she was going to sleep in. "Goldilocks would like this house. Everything is just right."

Grandfather yawned. "Well, Isabel, I hope you have a nice, normal bed in the guest room of your cottage." Isabel lived in a small cottage behind the big house. She and Grandfather would be staying there.

"Yes, I do have normal beds in there, James. Now let's duck out of here and let these children get to sleep," Isabel said. "Good night."

Ruff and Tumble looked up at Isabel. Then they plopped themselves down on the plaid dog bed in the middle of the room.

"Okay, okay. You two can have a sleepover in here," Isabel told the dogs. "But no barking when the clocks go off. Especially you, Ruff. And no climbing on these beds. Understand?" Isabel turned to the children. "I'll let Midnight out on the way down. We can't have her inside the house with these two."

Ruff and Tumble tilted their heads as if they understood every word.

"I'm not even tired," Benny announced

after Grandfather and Isabel had left. His eyes were bright and lively. He didn't look a bit sleepy. "I can't wait to hear all these clocks!"

Henry glanced at his watch. "It's almost midnight now. Five, four, three, two . . ."

All at once wooden birds and mice and even a rabbit popped out from the clocks in the room. They chirped and squeaked and hopped as they went in and out of the clocks over and over.

"They're cuckoo clocks, only with different kinds of animals!" Violet laughed with delight. "I've never seen such pretty ones, except for the Alice Putter nightingale clock at home."

The room was filled with chimes, cuckoos, and bells.

In the middle of the racket, Ruff and Tumble began to howl. Their tails moved back and forth in rhythm with the clocks.

The Aldens were still laughing when the birds, mice, and rabbits suddenly disappeared into their clocks. All the chirping and chiming in the house came to a stop.

"I don't think we'll be able to sleep through *that* tomorrow night," Jessie declared. "Not unless we get earplugs."

As the children climbed into their beds, Ruff and Tumble began to growl.

"What's the matter, you two?" Jessie asked softly. "Isabel let Midnight out of the house already."

"Listen," Henry said. "Do you hear that?"

The children froze in place.

Jessie shushed the dogs. "Tapping. Where's it coming from?"

With their tails straight up, Ruff and Tumble pulled away from Jessie. They stood at the door, whining.

"Something must be wrong," said Violet.

"Let's investigate," Benny said firmly. He led the way down the moonlit staircase.

When the Aldens reached the first floor, the tapping had stopped. The dim entryway was still. The face of the grandfather clock glowed in the moonlight.

In the dark shadows at the foot of the stairs stood Midnight, her back arched in

fright. At the sight of Ruff and Tumble, she ran out the open front door.

"Look." Henry pointed to the door. "That door shouldn't be open. The wind must have blown it open and banged it against the wall."

"I guess that's what made the tapping noise," Jessie said.

Ruff and Tumble tried to squeeze themselves past Henry to get outside.

"Don't let them out," Jessie said. "If they see the raccoon again, they'll wake up everybody." Jessie stuck her head out the door. The wind had picked up. Suddenly she gasped. There was a person in the garden! *Oh, it's only the scarecrow*, she decided. She pulled the door shut.

The Aldens walked back upstairs.

Except for the softly ticking clocks, the house was quiet. The sleepy children were quiet, too, except for the *thump, thump, thump* of their own heartbeats.

CHAPTER 2

Something Is Missing

The next morning, the Aldens awoke to the steady ticking of the clocks.

Benny's stomach rumbled. He opened one eye, then the other. Pushing his brown bangs from his forehead, he sat up. He was hungry.

Seeing Benny awake, Ruff and Tumble trotted over. They rested their quivering noses on the edge of his custom-size bed.

Benny stroked the dogs' long, silky ears. "You guys must be hungry, too."

Henry sat up in bed. "And I must be hungry three," he joked.

Soon all of them — boys, girls, and dogs — were up and about. Isabel had said they could help set up some of the inventions that had arrived already. The children could hardly wait to see what the other inventors had designed.

Under Jessie's supervision, teeth were brushed, hair was combed, sneakers were tied, and sleeping bags were rolled neatly on each bed. Benny put on his flashlight hat. Then the dogs and children followed their noses downstairs and over to Isabel's cottage. They could hear silverware clinking and food sizzling. The dogs ran ahead as fast as they could, which wasn't awfully fast on their short legs. Midnight, who was eating her breakfast, had plenty of time to scurry away.

When his grandchildren bounded into Isabel's cheery kitchen, Grandfather set down his coffee cup. "Morning, sleepyheads," he said, getting up to hug them. "I knew all these good breakfast smells would wake you up."

"Help yourselves to pancakes," Isabel said. "They're warming on the stove along with the sausages. Everything else is on the table. Now, tell me, did you sleep through all the clocks chiming at midnight?"

Benny speared a sausage. "No way! I stayed up *past* midnight! The clocks made lots of noise right in our room. And guess what. We heard some mystery tapping."

"Tapping?" Isabel asked, puzzled. "Are you certain it wasn't the wind?"

Jessie sat down next to Isabel. "I think it *was* the wind. The scarecrow was spinning in the garden, anyway."

During breakfast Isabel explained what needed to be done that morning. "Many of the inventors are already in town. Some have already dropped off their inventions in the old garage. Others mailed their inventions — you can help unpack them. My assistant, Martha, is registering the inventions now. After she finishes, you can help move some of the pieces into the main house. I'll meet you in the garage after breakfast and — "

Ruff and Tumble suddenly stopped eating. They skittered across the kitchen floor and rushed to another part of the house, barking all the way.

"Goodness, what's that all about?" Isabel asked. She quickly rose from the table to see.

Although they hated to leave their delicious pancakes, the Aldens followed.

"Mr. Percy!" Isabel yelled over the barking.

The dogs had cornered a short, round, balding man in the far side of the living room. A small wooden toolbox lay open next to him on the fireplace mantel.

"Please call these animals away!" the man cried.

Isabel and Henry took Ruff and Tumble by their collars. They led them to a small room and closed the door. The dogs whined and barked to be let out.

"You can come out in a while," Isabel told them. "Quiet, now!"

The dogs whined sadly. Isabel and Henry returned to the living room.

By this time Grandfather had introduced himself and the children to Mr. Percy. Mr. Percy didn't seem a bit interested in knowing who they were. He closed the door of a glass clock on the mantelpiece that had all its gears and springs showing. "Well, I certainly didn't need to be attacked by a pack of wild dogs, Ms. Putter," he complained. "If you want me to fix and clean your grandmother's clocks and artworks, you mustn't let those beasts loose on me."

The Aldens tried to keep from giggling. Ruff and Tumble loved to bark and whine, but they would hardly attack anyone.

Isabel tried to cover her smile with her hand. "I'm sorry they burst in here, Mr. Percy. As I've suggested before, please let me know when you're coming and where you're going to be working. Then Ruff and Tumble and I can welcome you properly."

Mr. Percy locked his toolbox. "I arrive when I arrive. I never know the time. Perhaps on another occasion I'll be able to finish cleaning the mantel clock without being attacked. I'll be on my way now. I noticed your grandmother's scarecrow sounded rusty last night. I'll go work on that. Just keep those dogs away from me."

After Mr. Percy had left, Isabel let out Ruff and Tumble. They yipped and yapped with joy. They were free to go back to breakfast.

The Aldens did the same.

Isabel sighed. "So now you've met Mr. Percy," she said. "I'm sure you'll meet him again. He's in and out of the house quite often, sometimes at strange hours."

"Mr. Percy had a lot of interesting tools in his toolbox," Violet said. "What does he do with them?"

Isabel poured hot chocolate into Benny's pink cup. "Mr. Percy is a wonder with Grandma Alice's clocks and artworks. He can fix or clean any mechanical object so it is in tip-top condition. But he shows up whenever and wherever he wants, without a thought to whether it's convenient or not. One night, he arrived at midnight so he could hear one of the clocks sound. It didn't occur to him to come at noon in-

stead. You should've heard Ruff and Tumble then. They did sound like a pack of wild dogs at that hour."

Benny reached under the table and patted the dogs' noses.

"So," said Isabel, changing the subject, "I thought today I could show you around the grounds and explain what needs to be done in the next few days before the convention starts. It sure is great to have you all here to help." She smiled at each of them. "While you help set up, your grandfather and I will be picking up the inventions of Grandma Alice's that collectors are lending us to display at the invention convention."

Grandfather put down his napkin. "Well, I guess by the time we get back Mr. Percy will have every movable object of your grandmother's spinning and chiming."

Isabel brought her dishes to the sink. "I'm going to go out to the garage to see what my other assistants are up to. You children can join me when you're finished. Just leave the dishes."

Of course, the Aldens never left dirty

dishes. After Grandfather and Isabel left, they washed, dried, and put away the breakfast dishes lickety-split just the way they did at home. Then everyone, dogs included, marched out to the garage to join Isabel.

"Wow! Look at all this stuff," Henry said as he entered the huge garage. It was filled with all kinds of gadgets. "I don't know whether to be excited or worried. I thought we came up with super inventions, but look at these." He picked up a pair of stretchy sunglasses that could fit any size head. Then he read the description of the waker-upper alarm clock. "There's a tape recorder inside. You can record whatever you want to wake up to, and the alarm clock plays it back."

"We could have Watch bark into the tape to wake us up," Benny said.

Jessie laughed. "He does that already without a special alarm clock."

Benny strolled off to check the other tables. "I hope nobody else thought up my flashlight hat." He patted his head to make sure his invention was still in place.

That's when Benny noticed a person reflected in the little mirror on his hat. When he moved to the side, so did the person. When Benny stopped, the person stopped. Benny turned around quickly. When he did, the man bumped right into him.

"Look where you're going," the man said.

Benny wanted to say something about the man bumping into *him*. Then he saw the look on Jessie's face. Benny swallowed his words. Sometimes having manners wasn't much fun.

As soon as the man left, Jessie put her arm around Benny. "Good for you. I saw him bump into you, as if he were following you on purpose. But it's crowded in here, so maybe that's why he was right behind you. He might be someone Ms. Putter knows."

Then Benny had a happy thought. "What if he makes hats? Maybe he wants to make lots of hats like mine. I'll be a millionaire and everything!" He was sure the world was just waiting for his flashlight hat.

"You never know," Henry said, pushing down the brim of Benny's hat. "I'd like one of those, too. Then maybe I'd have a chance of winning when we play checkers in the dark."

"There's Ms. Putter," Benny said. "Let's go talk to her."

Violet grabbed Benny's arm. "Let's wait," she whispered. "She's talking to that older woman who just came up to her. They don't seem to be having a very pleasant conversation."

Violet was right. Isabel looked unhappy with whatever the woman was telling her. Finally, the woman stepped away.

"I guess we can talk to her now," Violet said. "I wonder why she looks so upset."

Isabel's face was still red when she looked up and saw the Aldens. She could barely manage a smile. "Oh, there you are, children. Sorry I'm in such a tizzy."

"Is everything okay?" Henry asked.

Isabel nodded and lowered her voice. "I just had a bit of a disagreement with Martha, the woman over there. It's a shame, too. We used to be such good friends when we were children."

"You were?" Violet asked.

Isabel nodded. "Martha's grandfather and my grandmother were close friends, too. Her grandfather even rented this house when Grandma Alice lived in Europe for a few years. I'm almost sorry I invited Martha to assist at the invention convention. I thought she'd enjoy working around the house where she once lived. But she keeps forgetting it still belongs to my family. She often just barges in."

"I know we'd be upset if somebody used our boxcar without asking us," Benny said.

Isabel sighed. "I've found Martha in private areas of the property several times. I had to ask her for the key back."

The man who had bumped into Benny overheard this. "Good morning, Ms. Putter. If you have the house key, I'll take it to the hardware store to get it copied. Sorry I misplaced the one you gave me. I'll need another one so I can come and go while you're gone."

Isabel looked at the young man. "Oh . . . oh, that won't be necessary, Brad, now that the Aldens are here."

The young man frowned, confused. "The Aldens?"

Isabel seemed flustered. "Oh, dear. I forgot to mention they were coming. The Aldens are these lovely children, Henry, Jessie, Violet, and Benny," she said, sweeping her hand around. "They'll be staying in the main house and can let you in. Children, this is Brad Smithy. He's doing some work on the house before the convention. You can let him in anytime."

The Aldens put out their hands for handshakes, but Brad ignored them. "I can't count on these kids to be around every time I need to get into the house, Ms. Putter." He sounded impatient.

Isabel squared her shoulders. "I suppose I could postpone the repairs until after the convention — or find someone else to do them."

Now Brad was full of apologies. "Oh, no. Um, I didn't mean that, Ms. Putter. Sure, if these kids are around, I guess they can let me in."

Brad left, not looking too pleased with this arrangement.

Henry had a question. "So it's okay to let him in anytime while you're gone?"

Isabel nodded. "Yes, it'll be fine. Brad's done handiwork around here in the past. He's interested in inventions, though he hasn't had much luck with his ideas. He's a much better carpenter than inventor. He knows the house fairly well and where everything goes. Now I hope Martha has cooled off. I'll introduce you to her." Isabel called out to the other older woman. "Martha! Come meet the Aldens."

"Hmm," Martha said after Isabel had introduced everyone. "So you're all staying in my grandfather's . . . I mean . . . Alice Putter's house? Well, it certainly is a fun place for kids. You know, my grandfather was the one who gave Alice Putter the idea for the adjustable children's furniture in the kids' room."

Isabel looked startled. "What do you mean?"

Martha turned around. "Well, he built some children's furniture just like that for my sister and me."

Isabel seemed flustered. "That doesn't mean it was your grandfather's idea."

Martha stared at Isabel. "We *would* know for sure if you'd been more careful with all the plan books and diaries Granddad and Alice left in the house."

Isabel's cheeks grew bright red again. She drew in a deep breath before speaking. "My family saved everything we could find, Martha. Just because there's one particular plan book missing doesn't mean I've been careless."

"It's a plan book for the clocks that made Alice Putter famous," Martha explained to the Aldens. "Until it shows up, we'll never know what's in it." She glanced at Isabel. "Will we?"

The children wanted to say something to cheer up Isabel.

Finally, Benny thought of something. "Know what? We like looking for missing things. Maybe we can find that book."

"I don't think you'll have any luck with that," Martha said. "I've helped Isabel search high and low. Brad has, too. There's something about that plan book that Alice Putter probably didn't want anyone else to see. She — or someone else — must have hidden or destroyed it."

"Oh, I doubt that very much, Martha," Isabel said. "Grandma Alice was a very generous person. She had so many projects going, it's no wonder one of her plan books went missing."

"It's not a wonder to me, " Martha answered.

"We'll look for it," Jessie said. "What did it look like?"

"I have some similar ones in the library of the house," Isabel said. "Follow me."

Isabel led everyone into the house and to a cabinet in the library. She pulled out a large, flat book with a black leather cover. "Well, Aldens, if you're going to look for Grandma Alice's plan book, here's what one looks like. They're full of drawings and notes that Grandma Alice wrote down. She numbered each one. Number nine is the one that's missing. We think it contains many of her clock designs. Grandma Alice had so many places in the house where she stored things, the plan book could be anywhere. We've found all kinds of notes and riddles she wrote to herself about where she squirreled away things."

"I do that, too," Violet said, "so I'll remember where I've hidden presents. Once I forgot to write down where I hid some wool mittens I made for Benny's birthday. By the time I found them under my mattress, Benny was too big to wear them! Now I write down my hiding places in my notebook."

Isabel chuckled. "Grandma Alice was the same way. A few years ago, I even found a diary that mentioned a windup doll she meant to give me when I was little. She wrote a riddle about the hiding place. It took me years to figure out that she'd hidden the toy in an unused breadbox in the pantry! I do wish she'd left some hints about where that missing plan book might be."

Isabel put the book of drawings and notes back in the cabinet with the others. "You're welcome to look through these if you have the time," she said to Martha and the Aldens. "Just help yourselves."

"Are you going to search for the missing plan book, too?" Jessie asked Martha.

"I've never stopped searching for it," Martha answered.

CHAPTER 3

The Mystery Riddle

The next morning when Mr. Alden and Isabel came over to the garage, the children were already at work.

Grandfather looked on as his grandchildren worked. "You look like a colony of busy ants," he said proudly.

"We are!" Henry said as he and Jessie carefully set a large birdcage onto the pushcart they were using to move the inventions into the house.

Violet was checking that each entry included the inventor's drawings and directions. Benny was trying out a shoe polisher that worked with a pedal.

Isabel pointed to Grandfather's empty car in the driveway. "We just came over to say good-bye. When we come back in a few days, that car is going to be filled with Grandma Alice's inventions and artworks that collectors are lending us for the convention."

"Aren't you ever going to take off your flashlight hat?" Grandfather asked Benny when he came over for a good-bye hug. "You don't want to wear it out before the convention even starts."

Benny patted his hat. "I need it to see in back of me and in dark places, even when I'm busy."

"By the time we return, I may not even need Mr. Percy," Isabel joked. "You children are awfully clever at figuring out how all these gadgets work." She checked her watch. "We'd better head out now. I left sandwich fixings and fruit in the refrigerator, bread in the breadbox, and homemade cookies in the cookie jar in Grandma Alice's house. If you need anything else, just ask Martha. So long, now."

"So long!" the children called out.

"Okay, let's get these pieces into the house," Jessie told Henry. "I'll hold things steady while you push the cart." She admired the large birdcage, which was designed to look like a little theater. It even had a flowered cloth that lowered down like a stage curtain. "This will look pretty in the library."

Henry and Jessie balanced the birdcage carefully. They didn't want to disturb any of its moving parts. Violet and Benny ran ahead and held open all the doors. The older children rolled the cart into the house without bumping into any walls or doorways.

"There," Henry said when they finally had set down the birdcage. "That looks as nice as one of Alice Putter's own inventions. It fits right in. Let's try it out."

Violet turned a winder, and the curtains

came down. "Perfect," she said. "It works just the way the directions say. All it needs is a bird inside."

Benny wasn't too interested in birdcage curtains. He pressed a button beneath a globe, and the globe began to rotate slowly. When he recognized the shape of the United States, Benny pressed the button again, and the globe stopped. It was neat, but he liked his flashlight hat much better. Finally, he decided to see if there were any good books to read on the nearby shelves. "Kids' books!" he said when he found some colorful old children's books. "May I look at them, Jessie?"

"Sure," she answered. "Ms. Putter said we could use anything in the house."

To his delight, Benny discovered that all the books on one of the low shelves were for brand-new readers like him. He ran his fingers along the books. He stopped when he came to one with a missing spine. As he pulled it out, he saw that it wasn't like any of the others on the shelves. This one was homemade, with handmade drawings and handwritten instead of typed words. "Hey, here's a book somebody made," he said.

The other children came over to take a look. The cover was decorated with hand-painted clocks, birds, animals, clowns, and toys. There was no author's name on it. But handwritten on the first page were the words: *To My Grandchildren.*

"It's just a riddle book," Benny said, a bit disappointed that it wasn't the missing plan book. He read the title: "*Read Me a Riddle.*"

"So read us a riddle!" Henry said back.

Benny closed his eyes and picked a riddle at random. He opened them again, and read the riddle slowly.

> "*When the moon's at twelve o'clock,*
> *Pounce upon the stroke,*
> *The time to act is at the chime,*
> *When day and night run out of time.*"

"What's that mean?" Benny asked, puzzled. He handed the book to Jessie.

She studied several of the other riddles. "I know some of these already. But the one you found is hard to figure out." She flipped through the book.

Violet thought about the riddle. *"When the moon's at twelve o'clock* . . . maybe you can only figure it out at midnight when there's a moon out."

Jessie repeated the riddle. Maybe reading it again would make it clearer.

As the children huddled around the curious book, someone entered the room.

"What are you doing?" the person asked.

The children whirled around, surprised by the sharp voice.

Martha came up to the children. She stared at the book in Jessie's hands. "Who said you could take books from the shelves?"

Benny looked up at Martha. "Ms. Putter said it was okay, right, Jessie? I'm old enough to read. It's got riddles."

Martha reached for the book. "Riddles? Let me see it."

Jessie carefully passed the book to Martha. "Ms. Putter told us we could use anything in the house. She knew we would be careful. This book is handmade."

Martha was already turning the pages. "I can see that. Well, I'm sure Isabel wouldn't want such a fragile book being passed around. I'm going to put it away for safe-keeping."

"But . . . but . . ." Benny began. He stopped when he saw Jessie shake her head.

"I'm going to store it where it will be out of harm's way," Martha said. With that, she turned and left.

Benny took a big swallow before he spoke. He wasn't used to people being cross with him. "I didn't harm the book, right, Jessie?"

Jessie patted the top of Benny's flashlight hat. "Of course you didn't. But I didn't want to upset Martha."

"Maybe we can draw and paint our own riddle book when we get home," Violet said to cheer up Benny.

"That will be a good project for a rainy day," Henry said. "Now, let's just finish up a couple more things in here. We'll think about lunch after the clocks sound at noon."

Benny heard his stomach rumble. "I already have a clock inside me that says it's lunchtime. If we're quiet, you can hear it."

But the Aldens heard something else.

Tap. Tap. Tap.

"Where's that coming from?" Jessie asked.

Tap. Tap. Tap.

"It's going faster," Violet said. "What's on the other side of this wall?"

Jessie scrunched her forehead. "Either the big coat closet or the entryway, I'm not sure. Let's go find out. It's the same sound we heard last night, but now it's not windy out. It must be something else."

The children left the library. The tapping sounded closer.

Henry pointed to the closet door. "It's coming from in there," he whispered. "See? There's light coming from under the door."

Jessie went up and knocked.

"I've got my hands full!" a voice answered. "Just push if you need to come in here."

When Henry opened the door, the children found themselves facing Mr. Percy. He was huddled over a small table in the closet. He held a tiny hammer in his hand. On the table lay a bent iron hinge next to an open jewelry box, with a circle of dancers in the middle of it.

"What is it?" he asked without turning around. "This is delicate work. The hinge to one of Alice Putter's jewelry boxes is bent, and I mean to unbend it. Dust will get into the parts if I can't get the top to fit tight. What do you need in here?"

"Nothing," Henry said. "We heard tapping and wondered where it was coming from. I guess it was you with that little hammer."

Violet stepped closer to Mr. Percy. "That hinge is so small. Is it hard to tap it into shape without breaking it?"

Mr. Percy looked at Violet. For a second, he almost seemed as if he were going to show her how to fix the hinge. "Not if you know what you're doing and you don't have four children barging in. Yesterday, it was dogs, now it's kids. Can't a man work in peace around here?"

"We'll be quiet and still," Violet said in her sweet way. "I would just like to see how you fix things."

Mr. Percy pushed his magnifying glasses up on his bald head. "There's not enough light for a man to work around here with four other people looking on," he grumbled.

Benny took off his hat to show Mr. Percy. "Know what? You could borrow my flashlight hat. I made it by myself . . . well, almost by myself. Violet helped me sew on the mirror."

Mr. Percy put his glasses back on his nose. "Hmm." He studied the flashlight hat. Now he didn't seem in such a big rush to send the Aldens away. "Hmm," he repeated. He handed Benny back the hat. "I don't need to borrow it. I suppose you can stay."

"Thank you," Violet said. "I would love to watch what you're doing. I made a crayon saver for the invention convention. I think I need a thinner, longer screw to go inside the lipstick tube I'm using to hold the crayon stub. The screws from Grandfather's toolbox are too big. It would be fun to have lots of supplies and tools like you have."

Mr. Percy didn't skip a beat with his tapping. "Well, why would a child have tools like mine? These cost a pretty penny."

Benny reached into the pocket of his jeans. "I have a pretty penny." He hoped Mr. Percy would get the joke. "Here."

Before Mr. Percy could take it, the penny rolled off the table into an open cardboard box on the floor.

Benny bent down to find his coin. "Hey, why is this here?" he asked. "It's one of the invention boxes from the garage."

Mr. Percy stepped in front of Benny. "Leave that be!" He reached into his own pocket, then put a penny on the table. "Take this one. Now we're even. I don't want anyone going through that box or anything else in here."

Benny's mouth fell open, but nothing came out.

"No, now you all have to leave. I need to finish with this," Mr. Percy said. "You're blocking the light with all your heads and hats and such."

The Aldens turned to go out.

Violet looked back. She hoped Mr. Percy would help her with her invention another time when he wasn't so busy.

But Mr. Percy was busy. He cut a long piece of duct tape from the roll in his toolbox. He quickly closed the cardboard box and taped it shut. The box was sealed tight. Benny wasn't going to get back his penny, that was for sure.

"Boy, Mr. Percy works at the strangest times and strangest places around here," Henry said as he walked back to the garage with the other children.

"I know," Jessie said. "I wonder if he was working and making tapping sounds just like now that first night we were here. Don't forget he told Ms. Putter that he heard the scarecrow squeaking during the night."

"Maybe he just thinks about fixing pretty things and forgets the time," Violet said.

"Sometimes if I get ideas when I wake up at night, I want to get up and draw them right away."

"Then you need a flashlight hat," Benny said, turning his off.

The Aldens returned to the garage to tell Martha they were going to lunch.

Martha looked up from the papers in her hand. She was counting out loud: ". . . nine . . . ten . . . eleven . . . twelve. This is the third time I've had a box missing. How many inventions did you bring over to the main house?"

"Eleven," Henry answered. "I counted them."

"They all had the forms attached, too," Violet said. "I matched and counted every one."

Martha looked over Violet's shoulder. "Oh, Mr. Percy, there you are. What's that box you have?"

Mr. Percy walked past the Aldens, straight over to Martha. He handed her a cardboard box sealed with duct tape. "I found this in the house. Thought you might need it. Can't imagine why the delivery truck dropped it off there."

Benny looked at Violet with wide eyes. "But, but . . . " he whispered. "That's the box my penny fell into. Only it didn't have tape or anything."

Mr. Percy looked at Martha. "Well, the problem is solved." He walked away.

Martha checked her watch. "I'll unpack this one after lunch. I have to get going someplace."

The children started walking back to the main house.

"The problem isn't solved," Violet said. "Mr. Percy was nice to us until Benny tried to get his penny from that box. He knows we're helping unpack the boxes. What difference would it make if we saw what was inside?"

Henry nodded slowly. "All I can think is that Mr. Percy has something to hide."

CHAPTER 4

A Curious Phone Call

Benny kicked at the gravel as they continued walking back to the house. "I didn't get my lucky penny," he said. "Now it's an unlucky penny."

As the children crossed the front yard, Ruff and Tumble ran to greet them.

"Why are they outside?" Jessie asked. "Ms. Putter put them in the screen porch before she left."

Benny sat down on the porch steps. "Hey, you guys," he said to Ruff and Tumble.

"It's lunchtime for you, too. Where've you been?"

Jessie bent down to pet the dogs. "They got into the pond, I'd guess. They're all wet. I wonder how they got loose." She went to the main door. "I'm going to bring their dog dishes out to the porch so they can eat out here and not get the house all wet."

Ruff and Tumble tried to follow Jessie. They waddled over to her, ready to scoot inside where their food was.

"Let's bring our lunch out here, too," Violet said. "I feel sorry for them." She went over to the window. "Look, there's poor Midnight indoors. She'll be relieved that Ruff and Tumble have to stay on the porch." Violet leaned closer to the partly open window, where Midnight sat, staring at the dogs. Then Violet spotted something strange. "Come here," she whispered to her sister and brothers.

Peeking through the open window, the children saw Martha wandering in the en-

tryway. She had a book in her hand, and she was reading aloud from it.

> *"Half of me is part of the day,*
> *Half of me is clear.*
> *Pick me up, then turn me down,*
> *For passing time to appear."*

Jessie motioned everyone away from the window. "It's one of the riddles! The answer is *an hourglass*," she whispered. "Martha must have come in the side door just now. Didn't she say she had to be someplace? Let's wait a little bit to see what she does."

They didn't have to wait long. A minute after all the clocks stopped their noisy noontime sounds, Martha came out to the porch.

"What are you kids doing here?" she asked. She was empty-handed, but the children saw something sticking out of her jacket pocket.

Henry stepped forward. "We came to make our lunches. Would you like some, too? We would have asked you before, but

we thought you said you were going some-
where."

"I was, but it was noon, so I . . . " Martha
didn't finish. "I mean . . . uh . . . well, yes,
noon is lunchtime."

Benny looked up at Martha. Maybe she
would be friendlier if they all ate lunch together. "You can have one of my cookies
from the cookie jar."

Martha hesitated before speaking. She
seemed confused by all the Aldens standing
there. "That won't be necessary," she said.
"I usually eat lunch in town at the Red
Rooster Diner. That's where I'm going
now."

The Aldens looked on as Martha headed
to her car.

"Maybe she doesn't like cookies," Benny
said after Martha drove off. Then he
thought about this. Who didn't like cookies?

"You know what's stranger than turning
down cookies?" Henry asked. "Martha said
she came to the house because it was time
for lunch. Then she said she eats at the Red

Rooster Diner every day. She must have rushed over here for some other reason."

"Let's eat," Jessie said. "It's twelve-ten. Too bad we were outside when the clocks sounded." Jessie opened the door, then stood still, listening. "There's that tapping sound again — and a phone ringing. I didn't think there were any working phones in this house."

The other children stopped to listen. The tapping stopped, but the ringing didn't.

"We'd better answer that," Jessie said, stepping forward.

The ringing stopped, and a man's voice came from the kitchen.

"I guess you could say the inspiration struck at midnight," the voice said. "I just need to put a few more pieces together. The surprise will be ready in time for the convention."

The Aldens heard footsteps. They weren't sure whether to leave the house. When the oak door from the kitchen swung open, the children stood there like statues, facing Brad.

"What are you doing here?" he asked. "Are you eavesdropping on my phone calls?"

"No!" Jessie said. "We just came in to make lunch."

Brad stared at the children. "Well, come back in twenty minutes or so. I need to use the big kitchen table to finish a project. The light in the cellar is too dim for work."

Benny almost offered Brad his flashlight hat, but he didn't think Brad would appreciate it.

Henry was glad that he'd grown a couple inches over the summer. Just by standing tall, he could see over Brad's shoulder into the kitchen. On the long kitchen table sat a large wooden crate. Sticking out from the crate was an object that Henry couldn't quite identify — it looked like a curved frame of some kind. He couldn't quite tell.

Brad let the kitchen door swing shut, with the Aldens outside of it. Through the crack in the door, the children saw Brad push whatever it was down into the crate.

The next thing the children heard was more banging, only louder this time.

"He sure didn't want us to see whatever he has inside that crate," Henry said.

"*Yeow*," Midnight cried as she walked up to Benny and rubbed against his legs.

Benny bent down to stroke the cat. "Midnight doesn't want to wait for lunch, either."

Jessie looked up at the grandfather clock. "We have twenty minutes to wait. Let's see if we can figure out a piece of that riddle Benny read."

"Good idea, Jessie," Henry said. "That'll pass the time. Speaking of time, the grandfather clock is about to chime on the half hour."

Sure enough, at the next click, the grandfather clock made a deep rich sound when the minute hand passed over the six.

Violet stared up. "Look how beautiful the painted moon face is. Alice Putter was a very talented artist."

The children stood still, admiring the clock.

Suddenly, Henry smacked his forehead. "The riddle! What are the words again?"

"*When the moon is in the sky,*" Violet said. "No, that's not it."

"*When the moon is out at night,*" Jessie guessed. "Is that the first line? Too bad Martha took the riddle book away so fast. Now I can't remember the exact words."

"I know!" Benny announced. "*When the moon's at twelve o'clock.*"

Jessie hugged Benny. "That's exactly it! Hey, what if the moon in the riddle isn't a real moon? It could be something like the painted moon on the clock." She looked at Benny's excited face. "Do you remember the rest of it?"

Benny took off his hat, as if he were thinking so hard he needed to let his thoughts fly out. But this time, the right words didn't come.

None of the Aldens could remember the whole riddle.

"Here's what I do remember," Jessie said finally. "Ms. Putter mentioned that her grandmother used to write riddles to remind herself of her secret hiding places.

What if this riddle leads to a hiding place?"

Benny liked this idea very much. "Know what? Maybe the riddle tells the secret hiding place for the missing plan book!"

Henry stared at the clock face almost as though it were going to talk back to him. He walked around one side of the clock, then the other. He rapped on the bottom panel to see if it opened. "I just have the feeling Jessie is right — that the moon in the riddle might not be a real moon. And I have a hunch something special happens when the clock strikes twelve. If only we could turn the hands back."

"We might harm it," Violet said. "We'll have to wait until Ms. Putter comes back."

Jessie had another thought. "Or we could ask Mr. Percy. Oh, never mind. He acted so strangely when Benny looked in that box, who knows what he might do if we told him we wanted to see inside the clock?"

"What if someone else hid the plan book, not Alice Putter?" Henry suggested. "After all, Isabel has all the others. Just this one is missing. Let's just keep an eye out for the book *and* for who might have a reason to take it."

The Aldens thought about this as they went to the dining room to work. They moved dishes, plants, and knickknacks into a nearby closet to clear space for the inventions yet to come. The job didn't take long, even after they searched around for the missing plan book.

Jessie checked her watch. "Ten more minutes before we can use the kitchen. Let's check in the library room. It could be behind other books or in the closets."

"I don't see anything like one of those black plan books," Henry said after he checked a magazine rack under the window. "Oh, good. Brad's walking across the lawn. I guess we can use the kitchen now."

"Good thing," Jessie said. "Ruff and Tumble are howling for their lunch out on the front porch."

When the Aldens came into the kitchen, they went straight to the refrigerator. Inside they found a bowl of tuna fish salad Ms.

Putter had left for them, along with a loaf of sliced bread and a bowl of grapes and peaches. On top of the refrigerator was a cookie jar the shape and color of a shiny red apple. The Aldens liked apples just fine, but they *loved* cookies.

In no time, they had set up their sandwich assembly line the way they did back home.

"What does *inspiration* mean?" Benny asked Jessie. "That's what Brad said. '*The inspiration struck at midnight.*'"

Jessie cut a sandwich and handed the plate to Benny so he could put pickles on it. "Inspiration means getting an idea," Jessie said. "You know how sometimes you get good ideas about things when you wake up in the middle of the night? That could be what Brad meant."

Henry stopped pouring himself a glass of milk. "Or maybe Brad's midnight idea came from the grandfather clock."

CHAPTER 5

Noises at Midnight

That night Jessie stopped the clocks in the bedroom so everyone would get a good night's sleep. But it wasn't so easy to stop Ruff and Tumble from snoring. Their snuffly, wheezy snores woke up Jessie. She lay there for a few minutes, listening. Finally, she rolled out of bed and tiptoed across the chilly floor. *As long as I'm awake*, she thought, *I might as well visit the grandfather clock.* "Stay!" she whispered when she heard the dogs stir.

Of course, with Jessie up, Ruff and

Tumble wanted to be up as well.

"All right, all right," Jessie whispered. "You can come downstairs, too. I hope it's not midnight yet." Was she too late to hear the grandfather clock go off? She went out to the hall with her flashlight.

The steady tick of the clocks sounded so cozy, Jessie almost returned to bed. She aimed her flashlight at one of them. "Two minutes to midnight."

Like all dogs, Ruff and Tumble didn't need a flashlight to find their way through the dim hallway. They scooted past Jessie, down the stairs, and out of sight. Jessie started after them, then froze. She was almost certain she had heard a woman's voice coming from the first floor.

Before Jessie could decide what to do, the house filled with gongs and chimes and cuckoos. It was midnight again.

Jessie leaned cautiously against the banister and looked down. "It's Martha!" she whispered to herself. She watched as Martha aimed her own flashlight up, down, and behind the chiming grandfather clock. Martha appeared to be mumbling something, but Jessie couldn't hear what it was.

Jessie went down the last flight of stairs, not on tiptoes, but with firm steps. When she reached the last step, she aimed her flashlight straight at Martha.

All the clocks stopped at the same moment.

Martha whirled around so suddenly, she dropped her flashlight. It rolled along the floor. "Who's there?" she asked, blinded by Jessie's flashlight.

"It's me, Jessie. I woke up and decided to come downstairs. How did you get in the house? I thought I locked it."

"I . . . uh . . . it wasn't locked tight, I guess." Martha stood frozen in place next to the grandfather clock. "I left something behind this afternoon. I was just looking for it."

Jessie found this strange. "What were you looking for? Couldn't you wait until morning?"

Martha tried to get a better look at Jessie.

"I wanted to come get it before it got mixed in with all that stuff for the convention. Anyway, I've got it now, so I'll just be going." Martha bent down to pick up her flashlight, which had rolled into the corner. Something fell from her jacket. She picked it up quickly and stuffed it into her pocket.

"That's Alice Putter's riddle book," Jessie said. "Why are you carrying it around? I thought you wanted to put it in a safe place."

Martha patted her jacket. "This *is* a safe place. Now, it's late. It's time for both of us to go to bed."

Martha walked quickly out the door and shut it firmly behind her.

Jessie stared at the grandfather clock. "I wish you could tell me what your secret is," she said to the man-in-the-moon face.

The clock ticked steadily on.

Jessie went back upstairs. When her brothers and sister heard her come in, they woke up, too.

"What's up, Jessie?" Henry said in a tired voice. "Did the dogs have to go out?"

Jessie crawled into her sleeping bag. "No, but they woke me up with their snoring. I got to thinking about the man-in-the-moon riddle. I went to check the clock at midnight to see if anything would happen."

"I wish I'd gone, too," Benny said. Unlike Henry, he didn't sound a bit sleepy. "Did anything happen?"

Jessie zipped her sleeping bag to warm herself up. "I'll say — Martha was there! She was mumbling something and peering all around the clock. She tried to tell me the front door was unlocked, but I'm pretty sure I locked it so it wouldn't blow open."

Violet's bed was right next to Jessie's. She rolled over to face her. "Did anything happen with the clock? I was sound asleep, so I didn't even hear any of them go off."

"Nothing happened," Jessie said. "But Martha had the riddle book with her."

"That's very strange," Henry said. "I guess we should keep an eye on her."

"Guess so," Benny agreed. "Good night."

"Night," three soft voices echoed.

*   *   *

The next morning, the children finished all the work Isabel had asked them to do. Then they had time to work on their own inventions. Since they didn't see Brad around, they decided to use the long kitchen table as a workbench.

Henry tried on his rainy-day backpack, which he had invented for the convention. He had outfitted it with a special umbrella holder so the wearer could walk in the rain without having to hold anything. Benny warned him that it was unlucky to open an umbrella indoors, but Henry opened it anyway. "How else will I know if it works?" he asked in his sensible way. First it tilted a little too far to the right. Then it leaned a little too far to the left. Henry needed to make some adjustments.

"I'm not sure which of my two inventions to enter in the contest," Violet said. "My crayon saver is very useful, but it doesn't seem very exciting." She held up the lipstick tube that Mrs. McGregor had given her. Violet had put a screw inside to hold a small crayon stub that was too short to hold by

hand. "I wish I had some of those little tools and screws Mr. Percy had in his toolbox to get it to work better. I think I'm going to enter my jewelry arm instead, but I'm not sure yet." Violet held up the wooden hand and arm she had carved in art class to display rings and bracelets.

Except for needing fresh batteries, Benny's flashlight hat was finished. But he needed Jessie's help, anyway. He held out a wrinkled sheet of paper with his careful printing on it. "Can you read my directions so I don't have any mistakes?"

Jessie put down the screwdriver. Her invention was a convenient recycling wagon. She had built a small cart with two bins — one for newspapers and one for cans and bottles — that could be rolled out to the curb on recycling day. Jessie studied Benny's directions. "They look fine to me. Your printing is as good as your reading now."

The children heard the kitchen door creak open.

Brad and Martha stepped inside.

Brad set his heavy toolbox on the table.

"I have to work in here, and I need the table to work on. You kids will have to move your stuff to the counters. Don't worry, I won't bother any of it."

The Aldens looked at one another. Why couldn't Brad work someplace else? They weren't sure what to do.

Martha handed Jessie a box of fliers. "I need these posted around town, please. Since Brad will be working in here anyway, you can leave right now. Off you go."

The Aldens hesitated.

"Now," Martha and Brad said together.

Jessie and Violet carried their inventions to the counter on the other side of the kitchen. Benny kept on his flashlight hat, and Henry wore his rainy-day backpack.

As the Aldens left, they heard Brad and Martha arguing about another errand that needed to be done right away. The children passed the grandfather clock in the entry-way. It was ticking along in its nice, steady way.

"Just ten more minutes," Henry complained. "That's all we need to get another look at that clock when it goes off at noon. We may not know the whole riddle, but I have a hunch it's a message about this clock."

Jessie stepped forward. "I wonder if the glass over the face opens or if there's a panel in back or something." She pulled gently on a carved wood decoration that ran from the top of the clock to the bottom. "It doesn't budge, so I don't — "

"What are you doing?" Martha asked when she stepped into the entryway. "It's lunchtime. I think you should leave for town now so you'll have plenty of time after lunch to put up my fliers." She looked at her watch again.

Jessie's mouth opened, but her words didn't come out. She opened the front door and motioned the other children to follow.

As the children walked down the driveway, they saw a delivery truck on its way out.

"I bet the deliveryman just dropped off

more inventions," Henry said. "Let's take a quick look in the garage to see what came."

"After we're done, can we go to the Red Rooster Diner for lunch? I'm getting hungry."

Jessie smiled at Benny. "Me, too. That's a good idea. We'll check the deliveries, go to lunch, then put up Martha's fliers."

When the children entered the garage, they didn't see any unopened packages. What they did see was Mr. Percy. He was up to his elbows in packing materials — crumpled newspapers, bubble wrap, straw, and boxes with their lids wide-open. He was so busy unwrapping things, he didn't see the Aldens standing there.

"Hi, Mr. Percy," Violet said in her soft voice.

Mr. Percy still didn't look up.

Benny went over and stood in front of him. "What are you working on?"

At last, Mr. Percy noticed the Aldens standing there. He quickly put away a notebook he had opened next to him. "What are you kids doing here?" he asked. "I was just checking on these deliveries."

Jessie came over and looked around. "Ms. Putter asked us to do all the unpacking with Martha."

Mr. Percy closed his notebook and put a cap on his pen. "Martha rushed off into the house before noon — who knows why — and left all these packages just sitting here. Mechanical objects are my specialty. I like to look at 'em and fix 'em."

Henry went over to get a closer look at the inventions. "So what are these doodads, anyway?"

Mr. Percy didn't seem impressed. "A bendable spoon for a baby. Already invented! A combination snow shovel and broom. Nothing new there. A corkscrew-style garden hose that doesn't tangle. Invented already."

"You seem disappointed, Mr. Percy," Violet said. "Were you looking for something else?"

Mr. Percy stared at Violet through his

magnification glasses. "Of course I was looking for something else! Ever since Alice Putter died, nobody's come along with anything that could touch her inventions. Why, just look around this place — her clocks, her sculptures that don't just stand there. They move and do things. Things of beauty."

Benny took off his hat. "This moves and does things. Is my flashlight hat a thing of beauty, too?"

For once, Mr. Percy seemed about to smile, but not quite. "Almost, young fellow. Almost."

CHAPTER 6

The Red Rooster

After Mr. Percy left, the children put the new inventions that had arrived on display in the house. They could hear Brad working in the kitchen, but Martha seemed to have disappeared.

"I wish Mr. Percy had tried on my flashlight hat," Benny said. "People who fix things could use it, too. Or the deliveryman could use one when he's looking for packages in his truck. Do you think I'll win a prize at the invention convention?"

Henry was still thinking about getting

trounced in checkers. "Oh, I don't know, Benny. Suppose somebody comes along with a hat that has a fan in it or something? Or a hat you could put an ice pack in to stay cool on a hot day?"

Benny could tell Henry was just kidding. "But no hats came in those invention boxes."

"You're right," Henry agreed. "When you get rich and famous from your flashlight hat, just remember to send me one."

By this time, the Aldens were walking to the diner. Up ahead, they could see the wooden rooster perched on the roof.

"That rooster makes me think of chickens, and chickens make me think of egg salad," Benny announced.

Violet wasn't thinking about egg salad. She was still wondering about Mr. Percy. "Mr. Percy was so nice about Benny's hat today. But yesterday he shooed us away. I wonder if he was just having a bad day."

Henry didn't wonder about that at all. "Violet, you're too nice. If you ask me, Mr. Percy's hiding something. Didn't Ms. Putter say he shows up at all hours? And he was really weird about that box Benny's penny fell into. As soon as we weren't around, he started snooping inside the invention boxes. Looking at those boxes is our job, not his."

"I think Mr. Percy just likes seeing how inventions work so he can do a good job fixing them, especially Alice Putter's," Violet said. "He just seems absentminded about everything else except inventions and loses track of the time. That's what Ms. Putter seemed to think."

"I think he's nice, too," Benny said, taking Violet's side.

"Aw, that's just because he liked your hat," Henry said. "He's up to something. Remember how Ms. Putter told us he once came to the house at midnight to check the grandfather clock? That's pretty strange."

Jessie listened carefully to everyone's opinions before she said anything. "Well, Mr. Percy's not the only one visiting the grandfather clock at twelve. Martha's the one who has been spending time there lately. You know what? I think she figured out that the riddle we found has something to do with the clock. She even had the riddle book in her pocket the other night."

When the Aldens got close to the diner, Benny skipped ahead. He couldn't wait to eat in a restaurant with a big red rooster on the roof.

The diner was busy with the lunch crowd. Fortunately, with four pairs of sharp eyes, the Aldens were champions at finding empty tables. They made their way toward an empty booth in back. A waitress stopped by to hand them four huge menus. The Aldens were silent for a moment as they began to study the menu.

"It's hard to decide what to get in a diner," Violet said. "There's so much to choose from."

"You can have breakfast all day," Henry added, "even at lunchtime. That's what I like about diners."

"I like that diners always have big, squishy egg salad sandwiches," Benny said. "I've already decided." Benny switched off the light on his flashlight hat and closed his menu. He adjusted the hat's side mirror to get a better view. It was fun watching people walk into the diner through the door behind him.

"Hey," Benny said suddenly. His brother and sisters didn't pay him any mind. They were still reading their menus. "Guess who just came in. Martha, with a man in a suit. She doesn't even see me! Let's hide behind our menus." Benny was thrilled to be an invisible spy in the busy diner. "Guess what," he whispered. "She just sat down in the booth behind us."

"Who?" Henry didn't look up. He was still trying to decide between a turkey club and a grilled cheese sandwich. Maybe he'd have one of each.

Benny tapped Henry's arm across the table. He mouthed the name *Martha*.

Finally, the other Aldens realized what Benny was whispering about.

"Maybe we should say hello," said Violet.

Benny looked disappointed. Then something in the mirror caught his eye. "Hey!"

he whispered. "She's taking out the riddle book!"

"Here's the clue I told you about on the phone," the Aldens could hear Martha saying to the man sitting across from her. "If you compare it to these samples I showed you before, I think it proves Isabel has something to hide."

"What going on?" Henry asked Benny.

Benny adjusted the little mirror on his hat. "She's showing that man two of those black books Isabel got out of the cabinet. Remember? Uh-oh. What if one of them is the missing plan book we tried to find? Gosh, Martha looks upset. I wonder who the man is."

Martha's voice grew louder. "I just know this isn't Alice Putter's design."

Benny couldn't see the man's face in the little mirror, but he heard his words. "At first glance, it *is* convincing," the man said. "I may not be able to get back to you until after the invention convention. I have a lot of work to do before then. I'm one of the judges."

"Well, let's skip lunch so you can return to your office right away," Martha suggested. Benny saw Martha put the notebooks and the riddle book into an envelope. She pushed it across the table to the man.

The man took the envelope, then got up from his seat.

"Hey," Benny whispered. "They're leaving, and they didn't even order anything."

Henry laughed. "Don't worry, we're not leaving and we're probably ordering everything. Here comes our waitress."

The waitress passed the empty booth and came over to the Aldens. "Sorry I took so long," she said. "We sure are busy today. I guess the couple behind you got tired of waiting. They just left without ordering anything!"

"We know them — I mean, the lady," Benny said. "She wasn't hungry, but we are. I'm having an egg salad sandwich." Then he remembered his manners. "Please."

The waitress wrote down everyone's order and then left for the kitchen.

Henry frowned thoughtfully. "Doesn't it

seem as if Martha's trying to prove somebody else thought up some of Alice Putter's inventions?"

Violet couldn't bear this thought. "Ms. Putter would be so upset! Martha must be wrong," she protested. "All those bird clocks in our room, even the spinning scarecrow, all seem to come from the same artist. And so does Grandfather's nightingale clock at home."

Always sensible, Jessie tried to smooth out everyone's worries. "Whoever that man is knows about inventions — and about Alice Putter. After all, he's a judge at the invention convention. Everything will be okay."

"But what kind of clue is the riddle book?" Violet asked. "I wish we had it back."

Soon a tray of huge sandwiches appeared. The waitress's head was hidden behind all the food. She set down the tray and handed each of the Aldens a plate with a tall sandwich on it. Each sandwich was held together with a ruffled toothpick so it wouldn't topple.

Benny removed his toothpick and tried to take a bite of the egg salad sandwich. It was too big. "I can't figure out how to eat this," he said. The food looked so good, his mouth had already started watering.

Jessie handed Benny a knife. "Here, scrape half the egg salad onto your plate. Then I think you can manage the sandwich. We'll have the restaurant wrap up the extra. You can save it for lunch tomorrow."

"I'm eating my turkey and bacon club sandwich in one sitting," Henry said. "No leftovers for me!"

But Henry was wrong. When lunch was over, the waitress handed the Aldens a large brown bag to bring home. "Here are your leftover sandwich halves," the waitress said. "The cook put in some extra pickles. Oh, one other thing. Your friend left a business card in the booth. Do you want to give it to her?"

"Sure," Benny said, taking the card. He

handed Henry the leftovers bag to carry.

"Well, I guess my eyes *were* bigger than my stomach. I couldn't eat another thing," Henry said after he paid the bill. He pushed the door open to let the others out.

Benny walked out first, clutching the business card that Martha had left behind. "This was a good diner," he said. "We got sandwiches *and* a clue."

CHAPTER 7

New Clues

The Aldens strolled through town looking for places to put up the invention convention fliers. They soon found the town bulletin board and decided to post one of the fliers there.

Violet studied the business card that Benny had handed her. "What's a patent lawyer, Henry?" she asked. "That's what this business card says — 'Robert Marshall, Patent Lawyer.' "

"A patent lawyer is an invention expert," Henry answered. "They check if something

was invented already so nobody can copy someone else's invention."

"That business card must have come from the man Martha was at the diner with," Jessie said. "He sure sounded like an invention expert."

Benny frowned. "I hope nobody else invented my flashlight hat. Maybe I should show it to Mr. Marshall so nobody copies it from me."

Henry looked over Violet's shoulder to read the card. "You know, we just passed the street where this lawyer's office is. Maybe we could go ask him if he knows if there are any other flashlight hats out there."

When the Aldens reached the building on the business card, they were surprised.

"Hmm," Henry said as he pushed hard on the heavy oak office door. "I thought it would be a small, pokey office. This is pretty fancy."

The woman at the front desk looked surprised to see four children standing there. She smiled at Benny's hat, which was beaming right at her face. "May I help you?" she asked. "And might I ask you to turn off your hat, young man? Otherwise, I'll have to put on my sunglasses."

Benny whipped off his hat and kept it off. "Oops, sorry."

"We're here to see Robert Marshall," Jessie said to the woman. "My brother has a question about an invention."

The woman studied the Aldens' hopeful faces. "Oh, dear. I'm afraid Mr. Marshall isn't available today. He just returned from a lunch appointment. Now he has meetings with inventors all afternoon. This is a very busy week. The invention convention begins tomorrow."

In her nicest voice, Jessie tried again. "Would we be able to come back later when Mr. Marshall doesn't have an appointment? We have a special invention to show him."

Behind his back, Benny crossed his fingers.

Now the woman looked disappointed as well. "I'm very sorry. Wait. Here's a thought. Mr. Marshall will be a judge at the invention convention. Perhaps you can catch him there and show him your creation. He probably wouldn't charge his usual fee if you just chatted with him."

"Thank you," Jessie said quietly. "We'll look for him." She hoped she didn't look as let down as she felt. When she noticed some brochures on a table, she took one. "Maybe if we use our birthday money, we can afford a real appointment to show Mr. Marshall what we have." A buzzer on a small intercom interrupted her.

"Excuse me," the woman said. "I have to answer this. It's Mr. Marshall."

A man's voice boomed out of the intercom. "Give Martha Carver a call, will you, Mrs. Page? She's called me twice since I left her just a half hour ago. Tell her I'm busy all afternoon and I'll get back to her. I can't just drop everything to figure out riddles."

Mrs. Page pressed the button and coughed several times. "I have several people out here, Mr. Marshall. I hope you don't want me to say *all* that to Martha when I call her."

"Not that last part, of course," the voice boomed back.

"Anything else?" Mrs. Page asked.

Mr. Marshall boomed back. "Yes. Tell her I'll need more evidence. Alice Putter's actual plan book would help me a lot more than a book of riddles."

"I'll mention that when she calls again," Mrs. Page said. "Oh, Brad Smithy left another message for you. He said be sure to pay special attention to his entry in the invention convention."

"Brad Smithy!" Mr. Marshall yelled. "Every year he pesters me about his latest invention. He's not even a client. Some days I think I should retire and raise chickens instead of dealing with these inventors."

Mrs. Page laughed after she turned off the intercom. "Please excuse the interruption. Mr. Marshall gets a bit frazzled at invention convention time. I'm sorry we couldn't help you."

"We're sorry, too," Violet said. "But thank you."

"So long," Mrs. Page said.

"Mr. Marshall is pretty popular," Henry said when the Aldens had left the lawyer's office. "What do you suppose Brad's special entry is?"

"The crate!" Benny said before the other children could gather their thoughts. "I bet he's keeping his invention in there. That's what he was nailing shut in the kitchen. He sure didn't want us to see what was sticking out of the crate, either."

"I wonder if his invention is the surprise we heard him mention on the phone," Jessie said.

"Maybe," Henry said. "Brad wouldn't let me get near that crate. It could have been anything."

Violet stopped in front of a barbershop to put up a flier. "Mr. Percy and Brad both tried to hide things from us that were in boxes. What I can't figure out is if it has anything to do with the missing plan book."

Henry frowned. "Martha's the one I wonder about — more than the other two. She gave Mr. Marshall the riddle book. She clearly doesn't trust Ms. Putter. Plus, we've seen her wandering near the grandfather clock a couple times now at noon and at midnight. The question is, why?"

CHAPTER 8

Henry's New Invention

When the Aldens returned to the Putter house, they saw three parked cars in the driveway. They checked the garage, but no one was there. From a porch window, they saw Martha in the library room pulling books from the bottom shelves.

"Hi, Martha," Jessie called through the open window. "Need some help in there?"

Martha quickly stood up. "Wait, I'll be out in a second."

"Guess what." Benny said when Martha came out to the porch. "Your friend dropped his card at the Red Rooster. The waitress asked us to give it to you."

Martha looked down at Benny, then at the other children. "The Red Rooster?" She looked a bit alarmed. "Were you there?"

Jessie stepped forward and handed Martha the business card. "We were sitting behind you. You left before we could say hello."

Martha quickly snatched the card but said nothing about it. "Brad, Mr. Percy, and I are working indoors this afternoon. I have some outdoor work for all of you." She pointed out some large cartons and folded tables stacked on the lawn. "The rental company dropped off the tent canopies and display tables. That's where we'll put the inventions we don't have room for in the house. I need you to set up the canopies and tables."

"See what I mean?" Jessie said after Martha went back inside. "Why is she poking around in the house? There's so much paperwork to do with the inventions in the garage."

The children unpacked the display tents. They had done a lot of camping, so they knew how to put the poles together.

As the Aldens put together the tents, Henry thought of something. "These poles just gave me a fun idea! Remember that periscope I made in science class a couple years ago? I could make a few more out of these cardboard tubes that the tent poles came in. We can use them to see around corners."

Right away, Benny wanted one. "How about a periscope to go on my hat?"

Henry laughed. "You won't even be able to lift your head if you put anything else on your hat. I'm going to get our toolbox from the kitchen. I'll be right back."

"Go in the side way," Jessie advised, "Martha told us to stay out here. I don't want her to get upset with us."

Martha didn't concern Henry much. "I'll just tell her I had to run inside to get something I needed."

As he ran up the side steps, Henry heard tapping and banging sounds coming from the house. "Hey, Brad," he said when he stepped inside.

Brad looked up. "I thought you kids would be outside all day," he said. "Don't expect to work in here. I've got nails and my electric equipment going. No place for kids."

Henry grabbed Grandfather's toolbox from the counter. "We just needed some tools and materials. We're still working on our inventions."

More tapping started up in the entryway.

Curious about the sounds, Henry took a few steps toward the swinging door.

"Go out the way you came in," Brad advised. "Martha's in a bad mood about something she lost. Better not get in her way."

Henry hesitated. "Oh, I don't think that's Martha. She was working in the library just a little while ago. It's probably Mr. Percy. I saw his car in the driveway."

"Well, never mind," Brad said. "Just get yourself back outside. Martha's going to have somebody's head if those tents and tables don't go up this afternoon."

Henry returned to his brother and sisters. They had set up the tables already. "Here's the toolbox. Boy, people can't get us out of that house fast enough today."

Henry wasn't one to stay in a grouchy mood, not when he had a plan. Soon he was busy searching through Mr. Alden's toolbox. "Aha!" he said, and pulled out just what he was looking for — a tangled bunch of old eyeglasses. He spread them on one of the tables.

Henry didn't waste time. He carefully cut one of the long cardboard tubes into four shorter lengths. Then he cut a hole in the side of each tube. "This is the end I'll look into," he explained to Benny, pointing at the opening at the end of one tube. "But *this*," he pointed to the hole he had just cut in the side, "is what I'll see out of."

"How can you look in the end and see out the side?" asked Benny.

"By putting mirrors inside," Henry explained. "Watch."

Henry reached back into the toolbox and

pulled out several small old mirrors. "Perfect," he said.

"Thank goodness I didn't throw out the glass cutter that came with the crafts kit Aunt Jane gave me for my birthday," Violet said.

"Mrs. McGregor always says we never throw away anything," Benny said proudly.

This was true. The Aldens were savers. Good thing Grandfather had a huge cellar and garage, plus the old boxcar for storing all the things the children had to save.

Henry carefully measured and cut the old mirrors and fitted them inside the cardboard tubes.

"Done!" he announced and handed a periscope to each of his siblings.

Jessie squinted into hers. "I kind of see . . . oh, wait. I do see something. The dogs are on the porch."

Benny could spot Ruff and Tumble without the help of the periscope, but he still wanted to try Henry's contraption. "Wow!"

he said, peering through. "Hey, if I hold it this way, I can see things up high."

Periscopes in hand, the Aldens set off to explore.

Since Benny was the shortest Alden, Henry had given him the longest periscope. He immediately discovered a bird's nest under some porch shingles. "Everybody's flown away," he said to himself as he peered into the empty nest. He decided against looking any closer at a hornet's nest poking from behind some shutters. "No way."

Benny walked along the side of the house, turning his periscope this way and that to see what else he could discover. He decided to look through one of the tall first-floor windows. Balancing the periscope carefully, he gazed through the hole. The view he saw was a little wavy. It looked like the bottom half of a person. If only he were a little taller.

Benny ran over to Henry, who was using his periscope to look around a corner of the house. "Can you put me on your shoulders? I'm looking in a high-up window over

there, but I can only see half a person."

"Maybe whoever it is lost her head!" Henry joked.

Benny giggled. "I can't tell if it's a him or a her. I need you to boost me up."

"Ugh," Henry said as he lifted Benny. "Next time we do this, let's try it before lunch, not afterward. You feel as if you have stones in your pocket."

"I do," Benny said. "For skipping stones on the pond. I can throw them out if I'm too heavy."

Henry grunted. "Nope. I can hold you," he said. He carefully carried Benny over to the side of the house.

Benny held the periscope to the window. "It's Mr. Percy," he whispered to Henry. "He's tapping on walls. Uh-oh. He just went out to the entryway. I can't see him anymore. Okay, you can let me down. I thought we could see if somebody was sneaking around."

Henry laughed. "Somebody was. You! I wonder what Mr. Percy is up to."

Jessie and Violet walked over, holding

empty dog bowls. Ruff and Tumble trailed happily behind.

"I spotted these empty water bowls on the porch using my periscope," Violet announced.

"We can fill them from the outside faucet near the entryway," Jessie said.

"Good idea," Henry said. "You know, I like to see things with my own eyes. They're a lot sharper than my periscope."

The Aldens went to the side of the house, but the garden faucet didn't work.

Henry grinned. "Now we have to get water from the house."

"Let's just go in," Jessie suggested. "We can come right out as soon as we get the water." She walked over to the front door, pushed it open, and stood there, staring. "Mr. Percy!"

The Aldens couldn't believe their eyes. Mr. Percy was trying to pry open the front of the grandfather clock with a screwdriver!

Violet stepped forward. "What are you doing to the clock, Mr. Percy?"

"Please don't break it," Jessie said. It

looked as if Mr. Percy was trying to force the panel open. "It's one of Alice Putter's most beautiful clocks."

Mr. Percy faced the Aldens. "Break one of Alice Putter's clocks? I'm here to fix them, not break them. But this one has stumped me since the day I laid eyes on it. Every time I'm in the house, I puzzle over it."

"You do?" Violet asked. "I thought you knew about all of Alice Putter's inventions."

Mr. Percy pushed down his glasses and looked at Violet. "Well, you see, that's the great thing about Alice Putter's inventions, especially her clocks. Nobody knows everything about them, not even me. What keeps me going in circles with this grandfather clock is how to get inside the wood panel. It's locked tight — I can't get to the gears to clean them! I've tried tapping the walls behind it in case Alice somehow built it against an opening in the wall. I even wondered if there were a secret space or some such thing behind it. Can you kids figure the thing?"

Benny looked up. "Not yet. We're too afraid to touch it."

Mr. Percy packed up his screwdriver. "Well, if you think of anything, let me know. And good luck with your inventions."

"Thanks, you, too!" Jessie said.

Mr. Percy stared at Jessie. "Me, too? I'm not an inventor!"

"Oh," Henry said. "We just thought you might be inventing something, too, since you seemed so interested in the other inventions coming in."

"And since you didn't want us to look in your box," Benny added.

"I like to check out everything that comes in — I'm always interested in new gadgets and ideas," Mr. Percy said. "But I'm not an inventor myself — I'm a Mr. Fix-it."

"What about Brad?" Henry asked. "Is he an inventor?"

Mr. Percy sighed. "He'd like to be. I don't know that he can come up with anything original *and* make it work. But good luck to him." Mr. Percy looked up at the grandfather clock again. "Now *there's* an invention to beat! Alice Putter's last puzzle."

"Or riddle," Henry said after Mr. Percy went out the front door.

CHAPTER 9

The Search Goes On

The day of the invention convention was getting close. Thanks to Mr. Percy, Alice Putter's clocks ticked and tocked along. Soon Grandfather and Ms. Putter would be back. The children could hardly wait to show them the new inventions and ask Ms. Putter about the riddle book they'd found. They still had one more big job to do — finding Alice Putter's plan book. They kept on searching as they finished up their last-minute chores.

Jessie sent Violet and Benny out to

gather wildflowers to brighten up the house. She and Henry discovered a broom closet full of cleaning tools Alice Putter had designed. Jessie chose a feather duster shaped like a bird and soared around the house, dusting pictures, lamp shades, and Alice's many sculptures and clocks. Henry grabbed a dust mop that looked like an upside-down creature with a wild head of hair. He roamed through the rooms, mopping up dust and dustballs wherever he found them. Housecleaning had never been so much fun.

The hubbub was too much for poor Midnight. She moved out to the toolshed with the spiders. Martha didn't want Ruff and Tumble underfoot during all the preparations. She shooed them into a fenced area near their doghouse.

In between visiting the penned dogs and finishing their housekeeping, the Aldens did some final tinkering on their own inventions, which they had moved out to the garage.

"How will I show off my rainy-day backpack if the sun's blazing away?" Henry asked. The sunnier the weather forecast got, the cloudier he became. "I should have invented a hat with drop-down sunglasses or a shower that sprays suntan lotion."

"Maybe you should call it a sunny-day backpack," Jessie teased.

Henry began to laugh. "Okay, okay. No more teasing from younger sisters."

Thanks to Mr. Percy, Violet had decided to enter her jewelry arm instead of the crayon saver. He had given her an old music box part, then showed her how to connect it to the wooden hand. Now it played a little tune as it slowly turned, displaying the jewelry from all sides.

"Thank goodness Mr. Percy saves old things, too," Violet said. "Now I'm completely happy with my invention. Maybe I'll work on my crayon saver and enter it next year."

"I'm sticking with my hat," Benny said. "Mr. Percy said it's just right."

Jessie was oiling the wheels of her recycling wagon. To show how it worked, she had filled each of the compartments with old newspapers, cans, and bottles. "Yes, Mr. Percy turned out to be nice after all." She looked at her wristwatch. "I wish we had more time to search for Alice Putter's plan book. Maybe if we found it, Martha and Ms. Putter would get along better."

"Where should we look next?" Henry asked.

"In the kitchen," Benny said. "I want to eat my leftover egg salad sandwich. And from there, we can keep an eye on the grandfather clock when it strikes twelve. Maybe something will happen to help us solve the riddle."

"Good idea," Jessie said. The Aldens walked toward the house. "It's fifteen minutes to twelve now. That gives us time to drop off our jackets in our room before the clocks go off. It's getting warm out."

The children went through the kitchen, then headed upstairs. When they reached the first landing, they heard the front door open. Looking down, they saw Brad step into the entryway and look around. He set down his canvas tool bag in front of the grandfather clock then opened the glass door of the clock face.

"What's he doing?" Benny whispered, staring down at Brad.

"Moving the hands ahead!" Henry whispered back. "He's setting the time to twelve o'clock."

Just as Henry spoke, the entryway filled with the long, deep chimes of the grandfather clock.

The Aldens watched Brad in amazement. As the clock struck twelve, Brad quickly opened the wooden panel on the bottom of the clock with no trouble at all. The panel blocked the children's view. Was Brad putting something in the clock or taking it out? By the time the chimes ended, he'd closed the panel, then zipped his tool bag shut.

The Aldens looked at one another, wondering the same thing. How had Brad managed to open the bottom of the clock? Brad checked his watch. Reaching up, he quickly moved back the big hand eight minutes.

The clock now matched the others in the house. Brad picked up his tool bag and left.

"The riddle!" Henry whispered. "Now I remember it.

> *"When the moon's at twelve o'clock,*
> *Pounce upon the stroke,*
> *The time to act is at the chime,*
> *When day and night run out of time."*

"That's it!" Jessie said. "When the clock strikes twelve, the secret panel can be opened. Alice Putter made the clock with a built-in hiding place, then wrote a riddle explaining how to open it!"

"But what was Brad putting — or taking from — inside?" Benny wondered.

Jessie looked at her watch. "In eight more minutes, we can find out," she said. "I bet we can open that panel at noon, too."

Before the children could move, the front door opened again. Martha entered with the dust mop and a carrier full of cleaning supplies. She dusted areas that had already been dusted and mopped parts of the floor that had already been mopped. The whole time, she mumbled some words the Aldens couldn't hear. Every few seconds, she looked up at the clock.

When real noon arrived, the children nearly jumped at the sound of it. The whole house filled with birdsongs, cuckoos, chimes, and gongs.

Despite the happy racket, the Aldens focused on Martha. They saw her open the glass part of the clock. She ran her fingertips around the edges.

"Maybe she's trying to figure out how to open it," Jessie said. She didn't even have to whisper, since the clocks were so noisy. "Whatever the trick is, she doesn't know it."

Martha then tried to move the grandfather clock from the wall. It was much too heavy to budge.

At one minute past twelve, silence filled the house again. Martha picked up the carrier of supplies so roughly the feather duster fell out. She pushed open the front door, letting it slam as she marched down the steps. The feather duster lay in front of the clock like a bird that had fallen from its nest.

The Aldens were alone in the house. Noon had passed. They were a little closer to figuring out the secret of the grandfather clock. Something had been in there. Maybe it was in there now. Standing silently, the children looked at the smiling moon face.

"I wouldn't dare move the hands back the way Brad did," Henry said.

Violet nodded in agreement. "Mr. Percy said all of Alice Putter's clocks are very delicate."

"We'll have to find another way to figure out what Brad Smithy is keeping in there," Jessie said. She picked up the feather duster from the floor. "Or taking out."

Early that evening, during their light supper of tomato soup and crackers, the children heard footsteps in the entryway. Two figures appeared in the doorway. Grandfather and Isabel Putter had returned.

One by one the children hurled themselves into Grandfather's arms.

"You're back!" Jessie cried. "We've been so busy, the time flew by. But we still missed you."

Isabel stepped into the sparkling kitchen. "I noticed what a beautiful job you did setting up the displays in the library and living room — and under the canopy tents as well. I couldn't have done a better job myself."

After all the hugs were over, Benny took a piece of chocolate fudge from the box Grandfather had brought for everyone. "Yum. This is almost as good as the fudge we make with Mrs. McGregor. Now I'm full." He set down his empty milk glass.

"Our car is full, too," Grandfather told the children. "We collected several Alice Putter clocks and sculptures from the people who are lending them to Isabel to display during the convention. Wait until you see how beautiful they are.

Benny couldn't sit still any longer. "Know what we found?" he asked, jumping from his seat.

"Grandma Alice's plan book?" Ms. Putter asked in a hopeful voice.

"Almost," Benny said. "I found an old book with drawings and riddles for somebody's grandchildren. Only we're the grandchildren who read them!"

Isabel looked happy and surprised. "Oh, wonderful! Grandma Alice and Martha's grandfather wrote and illustrated many little books for us. They both liked silly rhymes, and both were wonderful artists. Sometimes they would hide something and make up a riddle to help us find it. Only the riddles could be very difficult, even for grown-ups. Where's the book?"

The children glanced at one another. It didn't seem like the right time to tell Isabel what they'd seen and overheard at the Red Rooster diner.

"Martha took it for safekeeping," Jessie said.

Isabel sighed. "Well, I can't look at it right now, anyway, we've got so much unpacking to do. Come see the treasures your grandfather and I brought back to put on display." She led the way to the car.

"Whoa!" Henry said when Grandfather

opened the trunk and car doors. "This looks like a moving van from a museum."

"Oh," Violet breathed when Grandfather opened a crate and pulled out a wooden clock packed in straw. "That is the prettiest clock of all!" she said.

The children came over to admire the piece. In place of numbers were carved vegetables. A woodchuck pushed the minute hand and a rabbit chased the hour hand.

Isabel carefully wound the clock. When the large hand struck the hour, bells rang. "I was quite surprised when I saw it. Unlike Grandma Alice's other work, I've never seen any photographs or drawings of it. It's very old-fashioned, the way clocks used to be long ago. No batteries, just lovely ticking and tocking."

At the sound of the bells and Isabel's voice, Ruff and Tumble began to howl.

Benny ran over and released them. They came running to Isabel, overjoyed that she was back.

Hearing all the yipping and commotion,

Martha came out of the garage. "Those dogs are supposed to be locked up. Oh, Isabel. You're back."

Isabel stood up from petting the dogs. "Yes, James and I came back with a treasure trove of Grandma Alice's work. We're about to unpack the crates and put the pieces on display in the entryway of the house, separate from the inventions."

Martha peeked into the crates. "How do you know for sure that your grandmother designed all these pieces? They're painted in more than one style."

Isabel sighed. "We've had a long day, Martha. There really isn't any time to discuss this right now. I see you have the registration binder. How many inventions are registered now?"

"Forty-five," Martha said. "Forty-six if you count Brad Smithy's. He's still working on his, so I don't have the paperwork yet."

Isabel pushed back a strand of hair that had gotten loose from her bun. "Oh, my. Last year, he had the paperwork but not the invention. Now he doesn't have either. Well, he sure seems determined."

Jessie and Henry exchanged a meaningful glance.

"Yes," murmured Henry, "but determined to *what*?"

CHAPTER 10

The Secret in the Grandfather Clock

On the day of the invention convention, Benny woke up first. He couldn't help it. A skinny slice of sunlight had squeezed under the window shade. That was all he needed to get out of bed. "Today's the day," he whispered to Ruff and Tumble. They instantly sat up on their dog bed. "Too bad you two can't go to the convention," Benny whispered. "I'll give you extra dog biscuits today."

The dogs crooned. They didn't know

about invention conventions, but they were experts in dog biscuits.

Benny padded over to the window. He yanked on the shade, which flapped up noisily. Sunlight poured into the room.

Henry covered his eyes. "Aw, Benny, it's not even six yet," he said after checking his watch. Tumble walked over and licked Henry's foot, which was dangling from his sleeping bag. "All right, all right. I get the message. You guys are like alarm clocks. Oh, no! Alarm clocks," Henry cried. "I forgot to wind the clocks in here last night so we'd wake up at midnight to try the grandfather clock. We slept through our chance."

Violet and Jessie sat up in bed, too. Ruff and Tumble ran over to Violet for their morning head-scratching.

Jessie looked over at Henry. "I forgot, too." She went over to the window. "We can always do it at noon. At least it's a bright sunny day for the convention."

Henry groaned. "Don't remind me. I'm submitting the rainy-day backpack on the sunniest day of the year!"

"I'm glad we finished our chores yesterday," Jessie said as she went from clock to clock and wound them up again. "Now we can go searching for Alice Putter's plan book before the convention opens."

"And figure out what Brad is up to," added Benny. "Hey, maybe he's keeping his invention in the clock."

The Aldens never dawdled when something important was about to happen. They dressed, rolled up their sleeping bags, walked the dogs, prepared breakfast, and ate it, all before the clocks chimed seven.

After washing and drying the breakfast dishes, they went over to the canopy tent for a last-minute look at the displays. There was Benny's flashlight hat along with a photograph of him wearing it. Violet wound up her jewelry arm. It played a tune as it turned, displaying the sparkling bracelets and rings Mrs. McGregor and Isabel had lent her. Jessie's recycling wagon was neatly organized and ready to roll.

"At least it was raining in the photo you took of me wearing my rainy-day backpack," Henry said to Violet. "Hey, it looks as if Martha put out a few more inventions that arrived yesterday afternoon. No sign of Brad's, though."

Benny tried on his cap one last time. He switched the flashlight on and off to make sure the new batteries were working. He put it back on the display table with the other children's inventions. He was ready!

The Aldens combed the house from top to bottom for two hours looking for the plan book.

"Whew!" Henry said. "It's got to be what's in the clock. But what would Brad be doing with the plan book? Martha's the one who acts so weird about it."

"If it is in there, then we need to keep a watch out for Brad and Martha when it gets close to noon," Jessie said. "Right now, we have to get outside. People are starting to arrive."

By eleven-thirty, Isabel's driveway was packed with cars. Henry kept busy direct-ing drivers to the parking area. He directed the driver of a shiny black car to a special reserved parking space. "Know who's in that car?" Henry asked when Benny, Jessie, and Violet came over. "It's Mr. Marshall, the invention lawyer we tried to see yesterday. He showed me his judge's badge. If we hurry, maybe we can catch him before Martha does."

Benny raced back to get his hat and put it on. "Do you think it's okay to ask him about it?"

But Martha had found Mr. Marshall first. The Aldens watched him hand her back the big envelope she had given him at the diner.

"He's shaking his head," Jessie noted. "Martha looks disappointed. The riddle book must not have proved what she thought it would."

Isabel and Grandfather walked over to the children. "Before the judging, I'd like to go over some final instructions with all of you and with Martha. Oh, she's talking with Robert Marshall," Isabel said. "Come on, I'll introduce you to him. He knows all about inventions. In fact, he's one of our judges."

The Aldens followed Isabel over to Martha and Mr. Marshall.

Mr. Marshall shook all of their hands as Isabel made introductions. "Alden? Alden? Where have I heard that name?" he asked. "Oh, yes, from my assistant, Mrs. Page. Would you be the children who came to my office yesterday with an invention?"

Benny nodded. "I'm one of those kids, and this is the hat I invented."

Mr. Marshall smiled. "Mrs. Page said you almost blinded her."

Is that good or bad? Benny wondered. "Sorry. I didn't mean to."

Mr. Marshall clapped Benny on the back. "No need to be sorry. Your flashlight baseball hat looks mighty useful to me. What good would it be without a bright light on it?"

Benny was beaming — and not just from his flashlight.

Martha was the only person who *wasn't* beaming. "Isabel, now that you're here, we need to get something settled before the convention starts. I showed Mr. Marshall these." She opened the large envelope and slipped out two plan books, numbers eight and ten, along with the riddle book the children had found, and a yellow notebook. "This explains everything."

Isabel pulled her glasses from her pocket. "What are you doing with those plan books? They belong in the library room cabinet. And what does Grandma Alice's riddle book have to do with anything?"

Martha looked angry. "This riddle book was not made by Alice Putter!" She looked at Mr. Marshall. "Robert, tell her."

Mr. Marshall shifted from one foot to the other. He didn't look happy to be there. He took the riddle book from Martha and turned to Isabel. "Have you read the inscription?"

Isabel took a closer look. "I suppose I did when I was a child. I haven't seen this book since then. It says: *To My Grandchildren*. Grandma Alice often wrote that in books she made and books she bought for her grandchildren. I'm confused, Robert."

"You won't be for long," Martha said.

Mr. Marshall looked as if he wanted to escape. "If you look closely, that's not your grandmother's handwriting, Isabel. One of my partners and I went through Alice's files in our office, along with these two plan books and a yellow notebook Martha gave me that belongs to her family. The riddle book doesn't match Alice's drawings or handwriting. What it does match is the writing and artwork in the yellow notebook. That notebook belonged to Martha's grandfather, Otis Carver. Martha told me he once lived in Alice's house. That might explain the mix-up."

Isabel still looked confused. "I'm sorry that the riddle book was left at our family's house, Martha. Of course, you may take it. But what does this explain?"

Martha stared at Isabel. "What it explains is that your family hid the missing plan book. You hid it because it proves that Alice Putter didn't design all the inventions she got credit for. My grandfather — "

Mr. Marshall coughed several times,

interrupting Martha. "Now, look here, Martha. Without the missing plan book, you can't prove that. Alice Putter was a very talented inventor. She and your grandfather had a great friendship. Let's not taint that with those accusations."

Martha glared. "If we had the plan book, I could prove them."

Before Isabel had a chance to say anything, another judge ran over to Mr. Marshall. "Robert!" the woman said. "I've been looking all over for you. You must come over to the displays right away. You won't believe your eyes! At the last minute, a young man just dropped off the most remarkable clock. Wait until you see it."

Mr. Marshall followed the other judge to the canopy the Aldens had set up near the garden. Isabel, Martha, and the Aldens followed along, too. A big crowd had formed around one of the display tables.

"What's all this?" Mr. Marshall asked as he made his way under the canopy to see what the commotion was all about. He had to show his judge's badge so people would step aside to let him through along with the Aldens, Isabel, and Martha.

Mr. Percy and Brad were standing in the center of the crowd. Brad was smiling and answering questions different onlookers asked him. Mr. Percy raised his hand to ask Brad a question as well, but the young man ignored him.

"Well, what's all the fuss . . . oh, my . . ." Mr. Marshall stopped and stared up at a magnificent wooden clock hanging from the canopy pole.

The other judge was staring up at the clock, too. "If I didn't know better, I'd say that looks like an original Alice Putter clock. It's so similar to the garden clock that a donor lent us. Except . . . "

"It's a clock *and* an outdoor birdhouse and feeder," Brad said proudly. His smile faded a bit. "Of course, I'm not quite finished. I haven't painted it. And there's still a bit of tinkering to do before it . . . works."

"Well, I must say, working or not working, this clock is charming," Isabel told Brad.

The second judge nodded in agreement. "I haven't seen anything like it since . . . well, since Alice Putter."

Jessie stepped in front of Brad. "Where did you get the idea?"

"I guess you could say the inspiration struck at midnight," he answered smugly.

Suddenly, Benny had the answer. "So *that's* why you needed the plan book!" Benny said, putting the pieces together.

Brad's face went white. "What are you talking about?" he said.

Jessie's eyes widened as she realized what Benny was saying. She stared at Brad. "Your clock is as great as an Alice Putter clock because it *is* an Alice Putter clock!" she said.

Henry glanced at his watch. "And in three minutes we can prove it."

"Just follow us to the house," Benny told the crowd, then took off running. The confused bystanders followed behind.

As everyone crammed into the entry-

way of the house, the clocks struck noon. A symphony of clock sounds surrounded them.

Benny bent down and carefully pulled on the grandfather clock's wooden panel. It sprang open immediately. Isabel gasped.

Benny switched on his flashlight hat, then looked inside the clock. He pulled out a notebook with a black leather cover and handed it to Isabel. "This is where Brad got the idea for the clock."

"Grandma Alice's plan book!" Isabel said. She opened the inside cover. "It's number nine!" She turned to Brad. "How did you know my grandmother hid the plan book in there?"

Everyone stared at Brad, waiting for his answer.

He turned away from all the curious faces. "From Martha," he mumbled. "I overheard her reading a riddle from a book. I've worked in this house for a few years now. Some of the old-timers who did work around here, too, told me stories about finding all kinds of crazy things hidden behind paintings, inside statues. One worker discovered a riddle under a windowsill he was painting. When he figured it out, it led him to a toy fire truck hidden in the broom closet."

"That sounds exactly like something Grandma Alice would do," Isabel said with a faint smile on her face. "And probably Martha's grandfather, too. I remember so many times the two of them sent us off on treasure hunts with just a riddle or puzzle to go by."

Martha stepped forward. "Take a look at it, Mr. Marshall."

Mr. Marshall took the plan book. No one spoke while he slowly flipped through the pages. At last, he shut the book. "This is Alice Putter's plan book all right," he finally declared. "But it's not hers alone. Many of the inventions in this plan book, including Brad's birdhouse clock and this grandfather clock, were planned by Alice Putter *with* Otis Carver. That's his handwriting detailing all the colors to use on nearly every single object. It looks like Alice designed the clocks and Otis painted them. The silly riddles written in the margins appear to have been invented by both of them. Of course, most of the clocks in this plan book were never actually made. I guess that's why you thought you could get away with this, Brad."

Brad looked away.

"So Grandma Alice and Otis created the inventions and artworks together," Isabel said, letting out a deep breath. She turned to Martha. "Is that what you were trying to prove?"

"Not exactly," Martha said. "I heard my grandfather tell stories about all the fantastic clocks and other inventions he came up with in this house. I just thought Alice Putter took credit for them. And I thought you hid the missing plan book so there would be no proof. I'm sorry I didn't trust you, Isabel." Martha looked sad. "We used to be such good friends and here I've been, sneaking around and trying to prove you had something to hide. I'm sorry."

"No, I'm sorry, Martha," Isabel said, hugging her. "If we had worked together like the Aldens did, we might have solved the clues our grandparents left us and discovered the plan book long ago. Grandma Alice and Granddad Otis would want us to be friends again."

"And we are," said Martha, hugging Isabel back.

Isabel went over to Brad. "But I don't think you and I can be friends any longer, Brad. You tried to pass off Grandma Alice's and Otis's invention as your own. I'm afraid I can no longer trust you to work here."

Brad looked embarrassed. "I'm really sorry. I know what I did was wrong." He looked at the two judges. "I guess I'm disqualified from the competition, huh?"

Mr. Marshall nodded sternly.

As Brad walked out of the house, the grandfather clock chimed the half hour. Mr. Marshall smiled at the sound of it. "I guess it's time to begin the judging," he said. "I haven't looked at all the other Junior Division entries yet, but I'd like to award Benny a special prize right now."

Benny looked up at Mr. Marshall and practically blinded him with the flashlight. "For what?"

"For solving the mystery of the grandfather clock — and looking inside it with your very useful hat."

"Here, here!" someone cried.

Benny took off his flashlight hat and waved it over his head. "Hats off!" he shouted. Then he walked over to Henry and put his hat on his older brother's head.

"Finally!" Henry said.

GERTRUDE CHANDLER WARNER discovered when she was teaching that many readers who like an exciting story could find no books that were both easy and fun to read. She decided to try to meet this need, and her first book, *The Boxcar Children*, quickly proved she had succeeded.

Miss Warner drew on her own experiences to write the mystery. As a child she spent hours watching trains go by on the tracks opposite her family home. She often dreamed about what it would be like to set up housekeeping in a caboose or freight car — the situation the Alden children find themselves in.

When Miss Warner received requests for more adventures involving Henry, Jessie, Violet, and Benny Alden, she began additional stories. In each, she chose a special setting and introduced unusual or eccentric characters who liked the unpredictable.

While the mystery element is central to each of Miss Warner's books, she never thought of them as strictly juvenile mysteries. She liked to stress the Aldens' independence and resourcefulness and their solid New England devotion to using up and making do. The Aldens go about most of their adventures with as little adult supervision as possible — something else that delights young readers.

Miss Warner lived in Putnam, Connecticut, until her death in 1979. During her lifetime, she received hundreds of letters from girls and boys telling her how much they liked her books.